MW0071466Z

WRITING WEST

WRITING
WEST

DOUGLAS
BARBOUR

Story for a Saskatchewan Night

RED DEER COLLEGE PRESS

The Publishers
Red Deer College Press
56 Avenue & 32 Street Box 5005
Red Deer Alberta Canada T4N 5H5

Credits
Design by Robert MacDonald MediaClones Inc.,
Toronto Ontario and Banff Alberta.
Typesetting by Boldface Technologies Inc.
Printed in Canada by Hignell Printing Ltd.
for Red Deer College Press.
Author photo by Fred Wah.

Acknowledgements
Thanks to the editors of the following, in which some of the poems have appeared:
*Aurora: New Canadian Writing, Canadian Literature, Capilano Review, Dinosaur
Review, Malahat Review, Secrets from the Orange Couch, This Magazine* (Canada);
Somewhere Across the Border, Poly: New Speculative Writing, edited by Lee Ballentine,
Ocean View Press, (USA); *Labrys* (Great Britain); *Landfall* (New Zealand)
Span (Australia).

Special thanks to Barbara Caruso for the drawings
which accompany "An Alphabet."

The publishers gratefully acknowledge the financial contribution of
the Alberta Foundation for the Literary Arts, Alberta Culture and Multiculturalism,
the Canada Council, Red Deer College and Radio 7 CKRD.

Canadian Cataloguing in Publication Data
Barbour, Douglas, 1940-
Story for a saskatchewan night
(Writing West Series)
Poems.
ISBN 0-88995-047-4
I. Title II. Series
PS8553.A72S76 1989 C811'.54 C89-091153-3
PR9199.3.B37S76 1989

for Sharon
&
for friends

&
for bpNichol (with love & thanks for the memories)

air   clouds   all
semes   gone   in

absentia   yet felt
aahhh   a sharpness in the air

inscribes   his departure
even deeper in the heart & lungs

body refuses to know this absence
phantom limb   phantom

breath   'you' hear as
his spirit ascends thru the city of clouds

CONTENTS

NOTES

MAYBE THE LANGUAGE SINGS
I. homolinguistic translation (one word per line) of W.B. Yeats's "Words for Music Perhaps."
II. homolinguistic translation (metonymic) of W.B. Yeats's "Words for Music Perhaps."

THESE FOR THOSE FROM WHOM
a series of poems engendered in that textual space where an image system of one Canadian poet intersects an image system of one SF & F writer.

EARTH SONG / BODY SONG
index of first lines
1. Robert Duncan, "A Poem of Despondencies"
2. Robert Duncan, "Keeping the Rhyme"
3. Robert Duncan, "Proof"
4. Robert Duncan, "The Structure of Rime XII"
5. Robert Duncan, "The Structure of Rime XIII"
6. Charles Olson, "The Green Man"
7. Charles Olson, "For Sappho, Back"
8. Charles Olson, "These Days"
9. Charles Olson, "The Ring of"
10. Charles Olson, "The Lamp"
11. Denise Levertov, "The Breathing"
12. Denise Levertov, "A Walk Through the Notebooks"
13. Denise Levertov, "Novella"
14. Denise Levertov, "Man Alone"
15. Denise Levertov, "The Poem Unwritten"

STORY FOR A SASKATCHEWAN NIGHT

for Robert Kroetsch

Picnic in a coulee in a cow pasture. . . .
But I couldn't tell a story. The
novelist unable to tell a story.
The ghost of my father, there in the
shadows–the story-teller.

The 'Crow' Journals
(Friday July 25 1975
Qu'Appelle Valley)

i

coyotes maybe hidden   nearby   i
am silent   the ghost in
the shadows waiting to speak   but
i am silent   listen

no   there is
no story   that
is what i have to tell you

i have to tell you   there
is no story tonight   there
is no story here   listen
there are all too many stories
clamouring   &
i have to tell you   i
cant tell them

9

if the cowshit could speak   it would tell you
nothing   no   well
nothing you dont already know
& the grass
talks on of dying   of dying
to feed the goddamned cows

        (this isnt narrative   hell
          its not even complaint

the flames die   too
& their story wont stay still
you cant follow
the changes   modulations

                      the sky
is full of stories   those bright
eyes looking down
on the prairie   i
cant begin to tell you   about

listen   all
the stories you wont hear
about that train now
its long roar fading
               in the dark

no   now that we know
theres no story at all
we can begin to tell it

listen

ii

what the silence said
was nothing   nothing
we could listen to

we could *hear*

the silence   it
wasnt saying anything
but stories   stars spatter
                on the night sky

that train   dopplers away
whooeee   WHOOOEEEEE
we hear that tale
everyday   each night
of its retreat   running
a storyteller   not
saying a word
into the dark   & away
from some
                place

or the cows
no longer seen   but
listen   their stories
are   shumpff mumchpht   chumpff
the chewing over of what vast
metaphysics   the grass
also refuses to speak
or the crickets

the writer   refused
        to tell a story
or   no   the writer
told us   he
        couldnt tell us
a thing   &

we listened   again
to the silence   no
silence   &

all it had
        to say

iii

or some other
possibility:

the yawning air
says   open
wide   theres a sky   now
swallow it all
                    empyrean

there   curved high above us
as the darkness deepens

more stories   appear
                            silent
insistent
          listen

          & sky
          tells another blue story
          of fucking sweet earth
          down there   way off   where
          they meet
          in utter silence as usual
                              (can you
                    see it   where
                    one darkness   solid
                    touches another   clear

                at the end of the road
                        end of the valley
                        end of the lake
                        end of the
                                        world

                or the story
so   far   away
& not telling it   again
of course

iv

the sky   opening
the land   the land   the sky

they keep repeating   they
keep repeating   they
have nothing to say   &
they say that   they
say   we say
theres nothing here
can you hear it

each time they
repeat it   each time
i believe it   i believe
theres nothing more to say

theres more nothing to say

theres more

                or   driving
            the point home   driving
            again along the prairie
            seeing what has not   been said

& saying it
s saying it

that theres nothing to say
& *that* grows

                          i said
            listen/
                    or look

its all around you
all those stories   you
want told
or it does

            listen
                    : one moon   only
                      a howling below

all that   empty   filling
with the stories we dont believe
we can tell

& we re telling them

V

plenitude   O
prairie   /   plenitude

                                        there is no room for
it unfolds   a short space   a
                                        short poem here   you
            nothing   must expand   to fill
                                        the space with words

is what it says

___
14

the sky   e g   un
folding   blue
                              no
thing   crisscrossed
labyrinths of cloud
unspeaking   un
speakable   grey   rain

the lines of
                    type perhaps
that rush against the window

nothing to say
the rain   says
dont   listen

the prairie   unfolds
so much   expressive shading
tones   say   in
spring   fall
a loss   or   abundant
shifts of   (tones)   mud
soaked in rain
fall   saying
                              nothing

                    stories   youll
never tell   yes

but who wouldnt 'sing'
either   saying only
i have
nothing
                    to say

ssshhhshshshshsh shsh sh sh

a few colours   hey
is it spring   or
fall   which
few colours   what
signs

that hasnt been said
or you werent listening
or it *wasnt*   a story

that time

it didnt hurt
you dont have to say
anything   you
mustnt cry

it unfolds   then
now   unfolds mystery

& that is what it wont tell
& that is what it cant tell
& that is what it
tells you

an abundance of
absence
you know

          say will be held against you
          all that   pain
          you cry   why
          me   so far from
          comforting   sky   or
          grassy hills   or
          not
          that horizon
          split with light
          a way   off

          silence

      you forget
      the catalogue
      of desire

      it grows

      the seeds
      grow   it
      opens
      wider
      it   refuses

      to speak

vi

this is   not
absence   simply

                      the presence
                      of absence

theres a story here   unspeakable
not to be told   i cant
                                tell it

nothing to say   of black earth
nothing to say   of the crops   tall
nothing to say   wind-swept waves
nothing to say   of wheat   say   the
nothing to say   harvest   coming

               in silence

            say   silence

            again

'THE WIND AND THE SNOW'

i

sunchilled

       lake a white expanse

moving
      the snow*
streams
sideways   below
over   crust
of   /   dunes of

white   (snow

    blowing

*we walked in it
   our noses raw, we sniffled while
      some one some
          where off the coast of California
  luffed sails, & enjoyed the weather
     & our rent
  but then   (& there
     who are 'we' to say this
  at the post office we were strangers
     & an other 'we'
           used to living on the lake
       gathered mail & took their
          children to the local rinks for
      this & that

ii

wind / word

in   or
outer movement of

wind/mind   blown
chill thru chinks of wall

that frozen   outside
moving inside*

here   & the furnace
forced   failing
to hold it out

that wind

*Who blows there ?   In what
 dark wood ?
 or wdnt   in
 the [k]notted heart
                of the flames

19

iii

snow blows
to the head   the world
bled white

               threads of
strife   rife
while the wind lashes the lake
                        ghostly

what shifting
             there below

'windblown'

that snow*

*out there   the
      shadows [of]   drift[s]:

"everyday"
           'i' *get*
                 "the blues"

iv

see   say
                    'solar wind'   or
a vision of cosmos

'galaxies like grains of sand'*
                              blown out   there

it traverses   centuries
          of white

wind across ears
                    years
                              blowing

about &
far

            theres that distance   &
            the few lights are
                                    stars
            in the far hills
                        dark
            ness falls on all
                        sides   for the
                        wind/blown
            seeds of
                        snow

or near   inside/
outside
          chinks of   (white

light   *swarms*

          *Doppler Shift: photo/graphs of distant galaxies
                    present a red snowstorm   falling
                        further
                              away

21

v

in the trees

surfsound

        (face freezing
slowly   red
ears   hurt*)

green waves
(above white   in
substant
       ial
          ity

windtossed

* Snowdeafness = white noise

22

vi

where language & landspace meet
flickering
before the eyes   the shift

of grains   of windblown
snow*

          an utter
fade

          into
what   opening   out
is all around 'us'

there

that white

          *that fell sometimes   at night
          white flashes in the cast light
               against the ever solid
               ifying dark,   "but"
                    as 'he' said
               "this comes gently
                         over all"

vii

there

watch it go
                    lightly

oh   yeah

there

that wind

that snow*

*photo / graphed :

    sunglaze off water
        frozen in time

    sunglaze off snow

RUMOURS OF WAR,
RUMOURS OF WEATHER

& out of the rumours what truth: his story: (told)/ invented .   last night in
this northern town i sat with a man & we drank beer .   talked fairly easily   &
he asked me how i write,   where does it comes from .   & i talked on talked on
till 2 more beers arrived at our table .   unordered .   an indian grinned at us .
held up 2 fingers   the man beside me waved   grinned back .   "a murderer
just bought you a beer .   smile .   got 4 years for killing his first wife .   dont
ever cross him ."

        & there was more: "he was drunk & something happened,
slashed her neck with a broken bottle .   then carried her 20 miles thru the snow
to the hospital here .   not the act of a man meant to kill his wife, no .   but she
lost too much blood .   i put him up in my cellar once .   not many whites had
anything to do with him .   welder .   hes OK,   but hes killed .   id be careful."
so would i .   i was .   thanked him politely when he passed our table,   new
(white) wife[?] on his arm .   not another word .

        walked to my room thru
falling snow,   the night bright with it   white floating over everything .

        woke in
darkness this morning   the snow still falling   caught by the mans act   that
long heavy walk / the reasons for it i wont ever understand .   i dont know the
man .   why worry about it .   but he has moved thru my night   & i hold
paper, pen,   white beneath my eyes .   outside my window the snow falls   &
it falls   to cover everything below   before men wake to mark it by their use .

out there:
the landscape he moved thru
& here   the paper
i write across

his trail / my tale
follows after

a blank,   a pain
blanketing the night
the forest,   the white
expanse   on all sides

shadows in the snow
that falls   & falls
soon will hide   all
below heaven   & man
s eyes /

            nothing
will staunch that flow
of blood   as he staggers
with his dear load   cut
by a drunken blow

the red flood paints their path/
                watch:

slow   so slow
he walks among the falling white
in bright night   wavering
south   (what bearing:
the greater weight?)
the snow   curtains
he continues to brush aside
for 20 miles   the red
trail goes slowly white
the red path dies
but he staggers on
bowed down /   what

can we know
of anger   or of love
that hauled him here
in this snow of confused facts
white landscape flowing
into a blank stare
their acts hidden there

he moves among the fall
& bears his load with stoic care
the air is bright with false promises .

the blood has stopped its flow
his path is hidden now,   he
cannot know this   the red
icicle scarring her neck
hidden on his shoulder / we
will never know   what he thought
of that long night
                              (nor those who judge

the hospital was eventually there
where he had known he must go
despite all,   his cold white load
deposit .   & the cold white
justice face .

but/   stare at the falling snow
see only these shadows
they move   slow   but
forever in
among the white,   the all
forgiving snow .

THESE FOR THOSE FROM WHOM

1   John Newlove & Ursula K Le Guin

meadow larks

the tree hates no one
as it sifts dimensions

    there /
         now
    here /
        then

tree translating **tree**
these shifting distances   &

melody

leaves whisper   or
the voices of blackthroats

I would be as
that tree   listening

not that one

the chrome crumpling   noise .
too much   the face

shocked flat

of that death

refused   *(refused)*

yet no hatred   yet

2 Margaret Avison & Brian Aldiss

Winter descending   always
now /   i seek
nothing   /   see
nothing as the snow
boils on the Yangtze
butterflies broken
on the starry wheel

i follow north   follow
no trail
across that country
this one   now
i dont know
when snow or
just ice   what
where i   began
now everywhere
this sun a full
white moon on pale sky
i stare at

& when discover

beyond that ridge of dark ice
crenelated   notches
the sheer fall of

time   gone
that creature

& here   o
hear me   the guns
glimmer fretfully &
yonder   against
the far off darkening night

the icy city glows tall
& cold   so cold
& bright it rises

3 Duncan Campbell Scott & Roger Zelazny

Dark moves
on methane snow

others move also in the stark
forests blossoming
frost   they
are alone   they
are   all   alone

are waiting
patient   their eyes
clear
above the soft fur
they have learned to wear
travelling snow
paths between
fires

now worshipped Dark
moves alone
with the light   the world
is changing   the world

is changing

4 Gwendolyn MacEwan & Vonda McIntyre

listen   this
shadow on black
sand   photo
synthesis   image
reversed   i
will ride you
o loving darkness

into a new
light
          dark
light

5 Archibald Lampman & Edward Bryant

'clanking'

it rankles   a
rank smell in
the almost empty room

high towers
stooped   &
keening in
steady wind
blows & blows &
blows the sand
singing within

there are these sudden
shifts of grey   or
more colorful knots of
people   passing
the time   &

there is that final
goddamn *clang*

the mind shutting
everything off

                    entropy

which is
to say   empty
it all out of
the eyes

he sits   now
he sits

now

6 Colleen Thibaudeau & Gordon Dickson

all those worlds
strung thru space   but
theyre only a pre/text

wander among them
'at a snails pace'
eons gone
try   to remember

but history forgets
all lessons
learned so slow
they never seem to
arrive at conscious thot

its been a long time
carrying the message
thru some speedy races
evolution   & no one
sees the writing
on a clear pane of glass
snails slime clearing
in the bright glare
a window of the pentagon
perhaps   the general
stares thru   or st peters
where the pope lies
dies always in state
so far above
the small shell on the floor

& that other shell
of apocalyptic news

empty now   & still
soon to fall from
the window sill

7 Daphne Marlatt & Samuel R Delany

how the nets work

the galaxies bright meshings
fall out   far-flung
seawrack   in a trawlers
haul   in
formation

they unfold   they
enclose   they
link us   bloodpaths
& neurons

shake it ripples   each
link tells
our civilization
is a   net ?
work the possibilities
or play them
                    (economics &   history   say
            what we eat out
                            tonight

the small boats ploughed the sea
reaped   sweet con
fusion of desire & luck
what feeds under
ocean   under
standing   the pier casts
its shadow   too

                    (or trees
            shadows
            net the light / sight
            falters in   in
            terstices of white
            & black   filigree of
            paving   sun & leaf

the connections   these
lights sign the skies with
messages   a mesh of
what 'falls from the air'
luminous map

what a japanese glass float
speaks of
bobbing among rocks near long beach
strung on a wall in montréal
other pinpoints on a map   a
cross this huge land

string them together   they
float a new imagination of

                (that other world   other
                    nets flung by nerve
                    into oxide arsenic seas

the web
weaves us all to
gether   gather
conjunctive necessity

right now   though
standing on a beach
late at night
look up
at the patterned stars
look down
                see them shine

nets   of light
language working
'the figure of outward'   inward

8　Al Purdy & A E Van Vogt

looking both ways
to the faint tracings   hung in air

    hung in air   luminous
    weaving of   aeons of
    human activity

& the empty atmosphere
of other planets   when

or here   but not now
one of us   perhaps
begins to swing
forward   & back   forward
& back

    look   you can
    see them   Klee folk
    moving superimposed   do
    you see   well
    feel them   sift
    imaginations dusty trails

    all those lives in
    glowing filigree
                here
    & somewhere   else
    so far   you cant
    count   nothing
    in the thin air
    of memory   meeting
                   nothing

meanwhile:
the stumbling starman trips
                          thru aeons trapped
behind a glass

all ways further back
& beyond   the clear helmet   stars
in strange patterns
                    now forgotten
traces of cosmic
dust   now
              nothing
                      waiting
                              to be filled

in the dream
it was written   this way   it was
a big
bang   it was
                  glorious

        these excessive distances
        in time   in space

        : to be filled   with

                          a word

9 Leonard Cohen & Thomas M Disch

a clever corpse is catching
angels

(not those in angles whirled

        inward & apart
        from the everwidening ring of song

      they are very small   & they dance
      forever on a multitude of pins)

but those others   dancing
elsewhere
who whisper melodies:

     this is better than sex
     the empty wasted body knows nothing

     not what its really *like*

        like swimming in grand marnier
           that delicious

        like fucking forever
           that far gone
           into flesh
           & out the other side

        (escaped   left behind
        now we fly
        a musical scale beyond human imagination)

lyric   lying

in my bed alone   again
now i dream   of angels

coming   & lost
        in love
           to me

10 Gwendolyn MacEwan & Roger Zelazny

"a repeated collusion"

the red bird you wait for falls with giant wings
transparent attack from the sky
blood salvation   one more day of quest
ioning is won thereby

heart in flight forward
                            pulse   pulse
       the story you tell
over & over   content
meant to hold   all
that moves

                "a strange muse"
you refuse that temptation
for a strange mood
comes upon you   Dis
cover   closure
is not what you want any
                 more

there are shadows   in
scriptions of your blood across
all routes from order in a jewel
        to a court amazed away
                        & in
between   that bird will fly
                    a telling
incident repeats
             all those versions of it

are you losing quest
or were you always
               there to
begin with at
         the ending
never ending
         words
worlds
     making the tale
              move

IN THE MIDNIGHT HOURS

Night time is only
the other side of daytime
but if youve ever waited for the sun
you know what its like
to wish daytime would come
& dont it seem like a long time
seems like a long time
seems like a long long time

"Seems Like a Long Time"
Ted Anderson (Talking Beaver Ltd)
as sung by Rod Stewart on
Every Picture Tells a Story

i

you enter them   alone   always
even if theres someone with you   you

enter them alone   thats given
you dont take it easily

                              its no gift
            (the dark)

                                    alone

breathe slowly   slow down   the images
behind yr eyelids   gather   they

are friendly   enemies
take them as you will
on the always nervy surface of
yr skin   yr thots

are showing again   you
breathe faster   know it   slow

down
you
go
          to enter the dark

its only the   dark

youre in it   as always
alone   &
breathing   like
a human being
moving in slowly
'one   breath   at
a   time'   asleep
                              again
                                    in the dark

ii

now   i would join you there   he
says   she says   the lover
                              says

& means it   wants to be *there*
try to share
whats yours alone
                    to bear

as desire & tongue always *wish for*
the pleasure not yet spoken   even
                              to give it
                                    language

loves us   but

41

there is too much dark

                              space
for words to cross
                        clearly
its lost in such translation

& yet 'i' speak   the poem 'speaks'
to 'you'
in the dark hours when once
youd have known   its

            only ghosts   or the wierd
                                    something wrong
            but wrong rightly in a world where
            such visitations come
                                naturally
                        supernaturally
                                    theyre expected
            & theyll pass

but no   the poem
isnt there now   with you
as it wants to be   poems desire
                                to transcend
the obvious   'im here'
the poem cries   you
cant hear it
                again

you have
                just ordinary
dark to dare   your mind   your
            light breathing   breasts
rise & fall   &

                        youre alone
as i said   not wanting to   not
wanting to know that   know you
are alone   where youve been before &

its all right   youll come thru   its
all right   not really   all right   but

its all right   for   now

iii

its midnight in the core of dark
lie down   &   listen

your last lost sigh   recedes
behind the song
                        ('i' send
in the dark   of the dark
you sing   it springs forth
it is the song of the darks own
you

& look
            you have
                        come thru

we usually do
make it   with
or without a little help
                        thru
                            the night

we always *enter*   alone
even together   to get
here   thru it
                counts   you
say hello   open eyed

the morning signals back the world
as you know it   as you know it
enter it   alive

MAYBE THE LANGUAGE SINGS:

I

1

Bring midnight in curses
dead was man

when banished
tomb as book cried coxcomb

God like safety
black hunch stood solid

virginity bids all
wanders under other man

2

the thunder-stones storm heaven
great lover   fol

elaborate   adorning
delicate joints
heart roaring   rol

3

Love unsatisfied
take body   Jane

take me
I scold certainly

Naked   my hidden black Jane
can love be but said

4

meet bone
leave love   but dark

lonely come love's body
leap in

left empty
ghost head
night dead

5

lover came   went
I come   remain

Banners   men-at-arms   horses
battle in God

their childhood
uninhabited suddenly to all

wild like men
body sings all

6

I said   breasts   veins
live in

fair needs
friends denied bodily pride

proud love in excrement
nothing has

7

image chosen   wound
scream bodily under love

she said   strike fate hate
love

die both
what limbs
dance love

8

I sing fancy   who
came   that upright   cried
was everything   young   old

9

change a heart
still   rage beat

throw glances bravely
fade crone before

that heart knelt   all offended
pardon

10

beauty awaits love
best lesser prove

lovers breath touch
touch love   lie

11

love wrote of wrongs enough   undying
heart hard
know rock desolate leaps

12

Old kindred ever stood
that blood throws thin
what thorn has torn

13

dreamed fathomless
my love's but the night burning

14

Plato's set Eternity unwound
and loves   take thread
break thread
bargain all

15

give bone all pleasure of bone
    women sang bone
      body gave bone
think bone when rightful did bone

16

Beloved   you were
Paris   golden   dawn
such wild being
leap and run
as upon holy
accomplished Leda   protecting

17

speech estranged under night
again Art is ignorant

18

shutter foul minds
know everything mad

there   below
page years unlettered   mist

makes me shudder
that   and snow

19

come   gone   that stone
body in the moon

sing what pleasure gave
sleeping   under
sun   moon

thought upon
man leans
until maid carry moon

20

Ireland and time come dance
      alone in man
      all stately is time   night
Ireland and time come dance
      fiddlers accursed   drums   trumpets
      and the malicious time
Ireland and time come dance

21

proclaiming men perfect
windy sang that cloud   proclaiming

22

sang under change
sight turned pure
and Holy
Wenching sing
something blinked in man
cock stands in faith

23

plain rhyme:
soul   Eternity
Time   world

24

perfection swelling
fail fantastic
                    stormy winding-sheet

25

Behold seas
beckons Golden blood scattered
through there
                there
                                Love

II

1

Dark & dryad   exploded
theories of heart attacks late at night
        (a possible lecture on the afterlife)
raging   for why
the corpse of him would speak of fools
        (Tycoon & town fool)

No diagonal man then   but
big enough to throw the joker out
        (a possible lecture on the afterlife)
beneath contempt   but bookish
quoting *Othello* yet
        (Tycoon & town fool)

The diagonal man the Other fucks
loses face in aging
        (a possible lecture on the afterlife)
signs of his impotence,   crippled
& ugly,   the Joker had roots, branches
        (Tycoon & town fool)

The Joker took me new
ups the ante   hard   would
        (a possible lecture on the afterlife)
darkly disappear
into comfort
opposing that, the Other,   reviled
        (Tycoon & town fool)

2

I wont listen to sea chanteys
of tempests not really meant;
a myth placed lady
transformed,   full of the same
old story
          (an old song

Bullish   & prostituting the science of
the *Inferno*
in love   always the bells hide traces
alongside the great name, goddess created
bars in space,   breakup
sounds always like give your all
shooting for the circle, move fast, metallic, outwards human
          (an old song

3

'We had it all'
or:
we should have had
the Coleman Hawkins version
          she said that

accept lemons say
getaway   create
that is   images
a sore throat   angry
words   soon over
          he agreed

undone   under
the stars   the sun
but where
          she said that

censorship   for &
against   (passion)
'if only'
          he agreed

4

an indian temple   perceived
in fear
others or i examine minds, moon forgotten
early passion lost
since they are only threads
spun between the light & the dark

by itself a phantom is only itself
arriving at the Other
but me, in passions winding sheet
jumping back as far as i can

always the self   separate
a typographical space
exercise Time,   teacher
training   ectoplasm
all tied up in the body
'in love'   again
out in the open
'the graveyard heart' insisted

5

the singles scene:
orgasm on his timetable
gone with the sun
no matter what i said
'here, there, & everywhere'
                    it all referred to the mother in the Other

old bones in armour
in the canyon
                    it all referred to the mother in the Other

'The House on the
Borderland'
                    it all referred to the mother in the Other

the Joker was my man
   i was his 'in
   a silent way'
   that music
                    it all referred to the mother in the Other

6

me & the diagonal man
on the way   talking
he spoke of the aging process
recommending the space program

    tears & anger: 'high
    & low   together go
    you know
    if youve lived whole'

theres arrogance
in rut   yet
passions home
is out beside the nuisance grounds
like the poet said:
    'what are we whole or beautiful or good for
    but to be absolutely broken?'

7

possibilities: Kurtzs ikon
heart-of-darkness woman
accepted everything he did to her
but I was afraid
       passion bites hard

or   she attacked him
death in both directions
me on the outside
       passion bites hard

where are they now
dead or   alive
I wanted them, no
I wanted to *be* them
       passion bites hard

8

'me, myself, & I'
all looking for that man

somebody else I saw
in tears   poor old bugger

another tune to play:
was it metamorphosis

9

the triple goddess
in the midst of transformation:
masculine craft within
once quiescent   older now
& powerful   the shaman
drumming   responded

look up,   send the spears
of desire to her without fear
for she is beauty
beneath her starry blanket
& eternal

before that truth
I fell down
that craft   over & gone
releases one   forgiven

10

'changes in latitude
changes in attitude'
passions falling off
          (a plea for refutation)

to make love
s to make death
come   closer
          (a plea for refutation)

11

nouns of eternal passion
verbs of purchase
inscriptions are tears
a question concerning price

a mixture of old clichés
reveals a solution
hope even
in the midst of despair

12

skeletons in the family closet
stand tall
the possibility of alienation
reinforces atavistic rituals

images from Munch perhaps
a statement concerning terrors
devious approach   via
the tenderest emotions

13

All those desires drilled
while I slept   close by
deep people arrive
thus the egos loss
Robin Hoods method
to put the spacing
where passion writes
hit whatever   second
or fifth,   the way
you do its powerful
metallic,   the expulsion
of breath,   & later
a new constellation
a conflagration

14

philosophy goes round in circles
according to this question
temporal misunderstandings
or sexual ones   what matter

but wait, 'I' am speaking
of agreements, promises
the labyrinth of galaxies

15

a plea from beyond the grave
          music on the coast
for future life, nurture
          its the Full Fathom Five & they play real cool

now a torch song
          music on the coast
a sexy blues too,   listen
to that climax
          its the Full Fathom Five & they play real cool

nostalgia, 'thanks
for the memories'
          music on the coast
is an alba   & it swings
          its the Full Fathom Five & they play real cool

16

this late night blues
for you   a kind of prayer
actually   wishing you
the joys of massive myths
with your miss

lover   you need your rest
even as the mythtaken
noble youth   drunk
& dead to the world
of happy animals
he no longer shared

that kind of dreamstate
joins uproar
terror   the time
the great bird took her
as ordained   & she
she took
care of everything else

17

it says its proper
to talk after such
prolonged speechlessness
but it also says
that in the safety
of 'a clean, well-lighted place'
'we' sing
about singing   of course
& the knowledge it brings
too late
stupid passion   gone

18

Get inside out of the storm
it hones my wits   &
now I comprehend
the worlds being
        – a kind of clouded anger

Look at all the famous
dead men
        inscribed
& once when we could
not read them
did we not know
        – a kind of clouded anger

so why am I so sad
even frightened
because I now guess
even the greatest knew
no more than
        – a kind of clouded anger

19

my music tells you this:
age brings decrepitude,
life in a garbage dump
    (the chorus is of precious metals
      the great exchange in the sky

you can swear all you like
but my music
knows that passion
& its products
always go gravewards
    (the chorus is of precious metals
      the great exchange in the sky

now I understand
an old timer
can say what he wants
my musics for everyone
    (the chorus is of precious metals
      the great exchange in the sky

20

This chorus is
too patriotic for words
even to the ballet

    singled out
    by his alien dress
    he altered his view
    spoke: of what was
    elsewhere
    & in darkness

This chorus is
too patriotic for words
even to the ballet

    shit, none
    of these people
    can play
    the simplest
    tune   nor
    keep time

This chorus is
too patriotic for words
even to the ballet

21

in the first person
tells us
what he did
for Jesus
(I think)

22

bloody cat
seen beneath the moon & stars
the same old question
concerning the losses of age

all these people,
named,   what
they did
or do
& still they die

everything in nature
seen at once by the Other
full of energy
'I believe to my soul'

23

a nightmare
in verse
'something like a Black Sabbath concert, I guess'
yeah,
& the lyrics are pretentious as hell

24

As if Oscar Wilde screamed
AIDS,   his beautiful ego
floating   some kind of glider
over pre-war Europe
writing some kind of science
fiction   I guess
inscribing death
& birth   in
that order

25

Another great mind
drowned
or buried
like the others
of the passion singers

AN ALPHABET

for Barbara Caruso

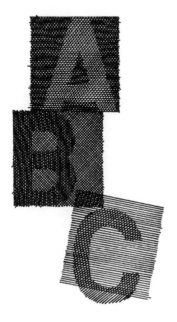

An action   act
ivity .   It
moves .   Me .

.

Barbara drawing .
It together .   In
tent   in
tense .   On .   Now.

.

Colours   shes drawn too

shes drawn to
                    colours
she makes with her own hand

more than   blue
never see the same blue twice

it flows   that
colour
they didnt even name

.

Determine
the line

       lines
drawn   in
drawn   out

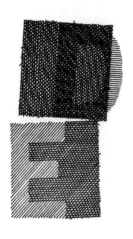

Desire   plain

thin wires of
desire .

   .

Empty the mind

Eye the page

Exercise
         (discipline)

   .

Further .
        in & out
to what is
         in vision   there

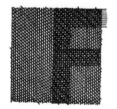

that is   there

           take it
slake it   care
is how the love
of lines full
filled .   & taken .
          in & out .

   .

Going beyond
colour only
long gone

it is the catch   minute
between
this colour & that
colour   &
that colour   colliding

no

conjunctive in this place
for the first time

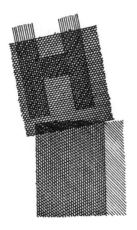

Heartlines

            bloodbeat
in fingertips
carving the delicate
traces of   (de)

lineation

Integrity of design .

Integrity of the sign .

In her
the gritty realization
of a particular truth .
                              Her
integrity .

Joy

of joining
lines &
colours blocked
together

joined
in
joy

Kaleidoscope stopped .

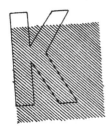

The whirled colours
of world
        arrayed
on blocks
        before our eyes .

Limpid

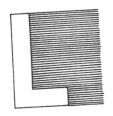

claritas of

the line

        spirit there

                (limpid

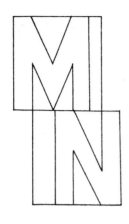

Make it new

Make it new

Make it new

Make it new

Make it new

.

Now .

.

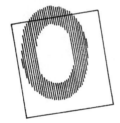

Open hand

Open form

Open heart

Open page

Open eye

.

Precision
            everywhere
pulse quickened
push of hand   of arm

position of line

picking a way thru inner traffic

paper there
pen

putting it freely in
                        action

.

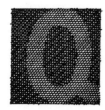

Quarrel with self

Question everything

Quiet   lie

.

Recognition:

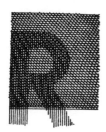

one swallows the world whole
in bite size slices

lines of occurrence
recurrency   & worth
every bite

.

Slow   down
        drawn   slowly   in
              to the world of colour

    or/   black&white
    contain them all

a grid
       of meanings   meaning

slow   down
read the world
           slow

.

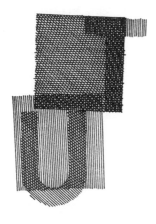

Tell
Tale
Traces

of what hieroglyph
      purity
          long   gone

.

Under   line

    (under colour
    under page
    under eye

what spirit moves thru

.

Vertical   (& horizontal
vision
      moves
         up & out   to
vast

.

White   space

waits

.

X-ray vision
almost   alphabet

extracted
from back
ground   grounded

lines emerge
across crossed lines
emerge

               thought
                                out

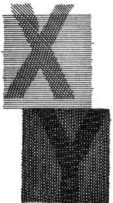
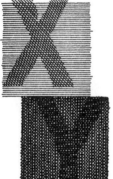

B.C.

.

Yes   it says
Yes   art says

Yes

.

Zealous
          in desire

(zebras track
the geometric veldts
behind her letters

written   with love
to us .

EARTH SONG / BODY SONG

i

We go whatever route to run un-
knowing   yet
knowledge is in sight   *in*
situ   this place we stand

at the end of the route
    rooted to the spot   &
                somehow knowing

        this is the message
        ive been sent
                    to bear

not barren
        the voice is full
the route is by the breath
    upwards   to the heart
                        the mouth

the seed of speech
    breaking   from the ground

ii

By stress and syllable
thru   take heart   &
haul   haul it forth

      that first you listen
      then begin to speak

love & touch are
speaking here   language

will languish
   lost to yr coming
if you refuse it recognition

    to say   i
    love you   &
    know the real

consequences are
never easy
      the words
only work if
you name them whole

every stress of
         every syllable
               felt

iii

For "wing of the bird" read
"desires rising desire"

    where   into what air
                will desire fly
      & what landscape
                         seek
far below

it is language desire enters
language it flies to
              soars over

    sinewy   sinuous
    the body of language
                    lies
    floats   sexual angel
        wings beating slowly
              awaiting   over & over
    desires approach

              your approach

do you love language   enough

    oh then   "wing
    of the bird"   fly

            fly

               oh speak

iv

My Lovely field! that into the Day comes. The ants have
this place   too   it
belongs to all
equal   before it

                we enter slowly
in procession
                    (as the ants   warrior
ants   on their long march   to
somewhere else
                    we enter

the ritual

do not ask   what it means
it means
        what you take it
to mean
            it is

remember   the field
is moving   we could be
standing still   within
or without

Day comes into it as it comes into Day

that is the secret of rime
                              (one secret

love is an other

love the field

V

Best of ways. That there be a law the Earth gives and the
poets know it   seek the law

elsewhere 'he' says   "The Law
I love is Major Mover"   &
what moves the stars moves breath as well
to rime

it has something to do with time
something to do with love
     (both words too burdened
     with meaning
     to hold their meaning still

yet the Earth does give
take & break as we will

there is time
          for love
& for rime

there is a hidden & lovely
law
          we breathe   & follow
     in the poem

vi

Go fool, and hatch of the air
some new desire   as
empty as the air
                  foolish
& undirected

the air is clear over the lake
    the lake is still
                  clean enough to swim in

but   desire   sometimes
"muddies the waters"
invites clichés
            & may be empty   a balloon
    easily pricked

but we are all fools
    sometimes   breathe
                  too fully   the heady air

the warning was for me
(me also

vii

With a dry eye, she
turned to another sheet

another lover   language
and another lover

    is it pain to see beauty   everywhere

    or simply worth the pain

some fragments remain
    to tell us
everything she knew
then   she knew
then   she knew

    & now we do
    too   *with a dry*
        eye   even some
            times   we do

viii

Whatever you have to say, leave
me something to wonder at
something unsaid

it shouldnt be too hard
we both have so much to say
these days

but everything!   no
that leaves no room
for intercourse
letting our talk match our bodies
sometimes

so tell me whatever
you have to say   &

dont leave
        yet
                dont
leave

ix

it was the west wind caught her up, as
    if to speak her name in
her flight from ocean
    to heaven   spell
it out   in the glittering stars

    who is she   she is
    desire itself   unleashed

she is that painting
& that one   that
           poem

    love rides the west wind ?
    or desire does   white
           waves rising   the wind high

youve seen her
in dreams   or some gallery
maybe youve read her
spoor

    language
    on the wind of
           the breath

    given to
Earth & her creatures

given

X

you can hurry the pictures toward you but
its you cant hurry to them

usually they wait
as the poem does

do not hurry
theres no need to hurry

theres need
in you
for the pictures
tho you may not know it

& theyre waiting for you
to see
them   read
them   as
they always planned you would

so many languages to learn
theyll wait for you to learn
wait   & you will learn

then the pictures will so close
with you   unhurried
so close   youll
meet them full

xi

An absolute
desire ?

    breath of
the mist
    sifting   thru trees

green is white
        ly meshed
the air moves
         almost
    to song

    my song
your song
    walking whitely
            into the absolute

silent dawn

xii

Let me walk through the fields of paper

Let me walk through the fields of breath

xiii

__In love__ (unless loved)   is not __love__
    denied ?   some lie
forsaken   some breath of
    honour died

     love died   they say
     meaning only   i died
          to love

language need deny
nothing
       love lives by
the words   the
     rhythm   the
        song

      of love
       so often lost   so often
found   again

xiv

When the sun goes down, it writes
    the moon   & stars
        across the sky

    such clear writing
    if the Earth intend to read

no clouding of the issue
the pure & profound
& always falling   further
into dark   night

    a palimpsest
        growing ever thicker
    as the huge radio
        telescopes peer further out
                (& in

a writing   a
    river   you
      never read
          the same way   twice

XV

For weeks the poem of your body
lay in wait
       silent

    i would read you now
    with all the care
           all the love   i bring
           can bear

"wild body of language"
says   our bodies longing
to be free

        our tongues
    speak on our bodies   writing
        these poems of
              desire

TWO WORDS / TOWARDS

To ward
off what
event   you
allow to
die into
any known
now .   Now
you say
it   now
you dont .
Night falls
in unrest
but all
the rest
is this
unknown silence
'you' call
thru to
'me' .   Why
do I
allow it .
I never
can say
goodbye   nor
why I
came to
you this
unknown way /
unknowing   pray
for some
new now
lost sound
of reflection
reflecting off
the water
to say
'I' or
'you' .   You

can only
say 'I
know what
you feel'
once .   Twice
now you
had me
at your
mercy, twice
you let
me go .
Now 'I'
would stay .
I would
say   Let
night fall
since all
you do
is go
away .   I
am lost
again: 'in
love'   I
might say
but you
wont believe
that .   We
hear as
thru a
glas darkly
doubled .   Why
should 'you'
care what
'I' say .
I say
what I
believe my
heart knows .
But who
knows anyones
heart now .
Now I

will say
it: 'I
love you .'
But who
speaks now
who spoke
before 'I'
said it .
I dread
it   seeing
I will
say and
never know
for sure
all that
I say .
And none
can say
precisely what
is meant
by that .
A retreat
to origins
of feelings
known only
in saying
and always
said always
before 'I'
or 'you'
say them .
This is
going nowhere .
Where can
'I' find
the first
beginning   beginning
what I
have to
say now .
I dont
know .   Know

only that
such knowledge
is already
spoken / written
down for
'me' to
ask it
questions .   Where
am I
going then .
Towards two
words that
must meet
in us:
this I
not 'I'
this you
not 'you'
will complete
some looked
for conjunction
only connecting
two words
to ward
off what .
Event .   'You'
allow it .
Lie down .
What is
said here
is hear
say .   Saying
again what
has always
already been
said .   We
are together
here gathered
to be
those two:
just 'I'
just 'you' .

A BAGHDAD JOURNAL

who

i

Sad man sad man whos saying whos sane when the sad man whos saying those things about us is saying them again & again to applause on streets & walls above the people everywhere that sad man whos saying this is what you must do in one 'photo opportunity' after another how many must die for a single mistake perhaps it doesnt matter the eyes of the sad man must see so much everywhere they gaze on the people at work & at play how sane can he be he has so much to do & its a damn shame he must bear the burden alone in the dark he has a vision a sweet river winding beneath a curved stone bridge the rich green of trees & bushes down to the rivers edge on both banks water gleaming in the sunlight in the darkroom he cant remember if he saw a man fishing from the bridge by the waters of Babylon some one sits still & weeps tho everywhere above the movements of traffic & troops he smiles or frowns on the action the sad man cant hear what hes saying over the applause for his name

ii

A sustained litany
                        shazam   this atman
is the breath of life

& the sad man whos saying that is
                         the madman whose sane objectives
reign over every satisfaction
                         felt thruout
the sand & oil of this country

There is a war
                    The sad man whos saying always
whats to be done
                    is aware of everything   he knows
His eyes watch over you
                    from every door & crossroads

what

i

The political gesture no one probably made this day in Babylon sun beating
down voice beating down on the crowd the minister of culture & information
sitting silent & reserved in his dark green fatigues in the noon day sun minions
dressed the same mustaches trimmed to the proper design of the sad mans pens
in the pockets on their arms the fight the battle of pens not guns today they
surround him would they throw themselves in front of him if someone started
running toward him he is important enough that soldiers check everyones
cameras when he delivers a speech but where in the midst of these bloody
festivities loud voices ranting in their chanting for the victory to come is the
quiet voice of the quiet memory the 20 flies buzzing on the ceiling the silence
after love in a city without pictures or applause i couldnt hear any of this in the
country so determinedly at war the poets are part of the troops with their own
front lines

ii

there is   no political gesture words alone can tell
there is   no political gesture unpreordained this day
                  in the blinding sun   in Babylon
                                          Babel is the word
                                          Babel is heard
              over & over   again as one
political gesture after another approaches the microphone

the sun shines
the general   [public]
              sits impassive
                          marking   time

where

i

In Babylon i heard the Goddess speak or maybe i would have heard that is i
desired it so much her voice a sibilant whisper in the branches of the Cedars of
Lebanon rustling across the rows of the amphitheatre & in the traffic sounds
maybe in between the calls & refrains of the market was she there to answer i
went to Babylon for her & she was there poets yelled it seemed names not hers
were taken in vain im sure i was listening i felt it i was listening i tried she
whispered in the sunlight maybe there had to be something in all that noise &
glitter the Goddess must still be there for someone even as the sad man leads
them all in some masculine name to war & in his name they all forget her she
whispered for me to hear i havent the faintest idea what she said

ii

On the road to Babylon
the last few metres
                        inside a glass cage
            the Goddess danced in various poses
                three inches high

                                    if she whispered
                    tho i strained to hear
                                    not a word i knew
                    even touched
                            my waiting ear

when

i

Walk then on a sunday afternoon streets bustling with business across the Tigris
only a few people moving about here near the mosque with the blue tiles thats
very beautiful take a photo of that be hungry its all right you missed lunch &
havent been eating much for a few days now anyway the sky is bright blue sun
high take it all in this city so new to your eyes & foreign as no European city
could be yet it looks like them too step out across this bridge across the Tigris
look downriver see beneath the empty sky tall hotels & wide gardens on one
bank those other buildings & thick walls upon the other get out your camera take
4 or 6 photos downstream pointing in various directions dont think walk on be
calmly happy as you walk above the fabled water & never hear the heavy boots
pounding behind you suddenly seized be yelled at in Arabic utterly afraid of
these grim young men in uniform their Uzi sub-machine guns in their hands
grabbing you by the arms & hustling you back to a gatehouse under the bridge
try not to show your fear wait sweating in the sun while camera & passport
travel a confused trail to some officer somewhere further in where some english
may be spoken yes wait hope perhaps eventually theyll just take the film smile &
explain "Fort Knock" & let you go tired hungry still very frightened walking
back across that bridge staring straight ahead never once pausing to gaze along
the ancient river banks

ii

final day   no passage
thru languages barrier
the photo not taken
but the threat seen

an hour in that company   too long
            a silence
                    'what have i done wrong?'

the sun fierce
as the boys in green with guns

nothing happened
one roll of film confiscated
an explanation lost in translation

a long walk across the Tigris
            the magic of that name lost too
in a dark transformation

why

i

You see we are trying to haul ourselves from the fourteenth into the twentieth
century in one generation & into the late twentieth century too one hand on the
wheel one hand gesturing then hitting the horn as he shifts lanes with what
seems reckless abandon but everyone drives that way here its crazy tho weve
seen no accidents heard of none heard only the busy conversation of horns roar
of acceleration everywhere they drive as their ancestors rode the desert of course
its the sad man whos saying this the sad man whos seen the light of an oil lamp
& the map he draws draws his country ever faster into the ever faster whirl of the
century of technological progress he knows hes right theres only so much oil
only so much time surely Allah wills it he listens for a word but its hard to hear
anything over all that applause & gunfire its a very complex exceedingly
difficult effort the future is a highway stretching out across the red desert sands
drive hes saying in Allahs name look out where youre going

ii

We are trying to bring our country from the 14th to the late 20th
century in one massive motion
                                        he drives one-handed   looking
back to speak to us
                              we cannot see what lies beyond
his headlights in the gathering dark

95

how

i

As a tourist only as a tourist unknowing knowing only how much he doesnt
understand he is on tour in this country so unlike his own & just like a tourist he
is taking photographs again how many has he taken already he has taken in the
suk with new companions & the road to Babylon the fabulous archeological
excavations there the other writers from around the world all gathered to
celebrate what he isnt sure they call it poetry the Tigris brown & majestically
slow slides thru the city it is a name to conjure with a name so full of ancient
myth & history & now the same international modern hirises tower along its
banks & he can see the American standard hotels thrusting above the low
whitewashed houses along the embankment from where he stands on the bridge
arching over this fabled name flowing below a snap/shot & another down the
river he walks on & is flustered then frightened when the green uniformed
youths with their automatic rifles yell at him in a foreign tongue point at his
camera & haul him off to sit for an hour or more in the hot sun until an older
officer explains in halting english that no one is allowed to take photographs
there give us the film please holding his camera oh yes he is happy (unhappy) to
do so (to lose all his shots of the suk) sorry yes he is free to walk across the
bridge again staring straight ahead staring surreptitiously at the many large
thickly concrete buildings what exactly is that place he is only a tourist after all
& no one is saying precisely what it is but it is army or government they are the
same even for a tourist youve gotta be careful where you aim your camera
around here lucky for you you were Canadian another tourist says

ii

As a tourist
only
Doesnt know the first goddam thing about the place
does he
No   (Know)
is looking
hard   at everything

taking it in
& home

just like a bloody tourist
yeah